WILL I EVER BE OLDER?

by Eva Grant

illustrated by Susan Lexa

Chariot Books
DAVID C. COOK PUBLISHING CO.

Steven was born before I was. He's so lucky.

Now he's ten. I'm seven. When he's eleven, I'll be eight. Even when he's thirty-three, I'll only be thirty.

I'll never catch up to him.

I hardly ever get new clothes.

When Steven gets new shirts, I get his old ones. When he gets new jeans, I get his old jeans.

Sometimes his old jeans have a patch on them. I *hate* wearing jeans with patches.

I get Steven's old soccer shoes. And his old soccer ball.

I get his old roller skates — without a skate key.

I even get his old teachers.

Sometimes Ms. Hardy says, "David, why can't you be more like your brother? Steven was hardly ever late to school."

Or, "Steven would never talk to me like that."

Or, "Steven always had his homework done. Why don't you?"

9

Sometimes people don't even seem to remember my name.

Once in a while Grandma calls me Steven.

"I'm *David*," I tell her.

But she forgets. "Come here, Steven," she says.

11

It's things like that that make me sometimes wish there *were* no Steven.

Last week, Mom and I drove over to pick Steven up after his soccer practice. He wasn't waiting for us where he should have been.

Mom was worried, but I wasn't.

"Maybe we'll never find him," I said. "And then I'll get to be the oldest."

Mom gave me a funny look.

13

Then I asked, "Mom, do you think I will ever be older than Steven?" I knew it was kind of a silly question, but it's something I always wonder about.

"No," Mom said gently. "But maybe being the oldest isn't always so great."

"What do you mean?"

"When Steven was born," Mom said, "Dad and I didn't know much about taking care of babies. We sort of practiced on Steven, and we were really nervous. But when you came along, you were lots of fun."

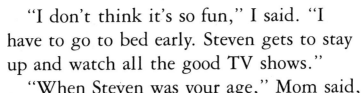

"I don't think it's so fun," I said. "I have to go to bed early. Steven gets to stay up and watch all the good TV shows."

"When Steven was your age," Mom said, "he had to go to bed earlier than you do now."

"I don't think Steven ever was my age," I grumbled. But Mom kept talking.

"Have you ever noticed that Steven has more chores to do than you do? There's more work when you get older. I stay up even later than Steven does. But I have more jobs, too — like doing the family's bills."

17

"Now, the Bible says there's a right time to be born," Mom said. "God planned for Steven *and* for you. . . . Where is Steven, anyway?" She looked worried.

I wasn't worried, but I was getting tired of sitting around. So I said, "I'll go and see if I can find Steven in the locker room."

"Thank you, David," Mom said.

As I ran up the walk, I thought about Steven and the soccer team. You had to be eight years old to join the team. It was just one more thing I was too young to do.

19

Then I saw Steven running down the walk toward me.

"Where's Mom?" he shouted. "I can't wait to tell her the news!"

Without waiting for me to answer, he ran right past me, almost knocking me over.

I followed Steven as he took my place on the bench.

"Mom," said Steven, "I've been asked to go to a soccer clinic!"

"What's a clinic?" I asked.

Steven didn't even look at me. He just kept talking to Mom. "It's two whole days of doing nothing but playing soccer," he said. "A famous soccer player is going to give us tips on playing better soccer. Can I go, Mom? Please?"

Mom looked at me. "When is the clinic, and who can go?" she asked.

"It's this weekend," said Steven. "And it's only for team members."

23

Steven left early Saturday morning.
Mom and Dad said that while Steven was
gone, we could pretend I was older. First
Dad gave me Steven's job: raking leaves.
After I finished, I kicked around Steven's
old soccer ball for a while. But there was
no one to kick it back to me.

On Saturday night, I got to stay up late to watch a TV program. It was one of Steven's favorite shows, but he wasn't there to laugh at it with me.

After church Sunday, Mom made one of my favorite meals. "I love you lots!" she whispered. But dinner seemed too quiet.

27

Finally Steven came home. He was full of funny stories about the clinic, and he kept all of us laughing for a long time — even me. I was surprised at how nice it felt to have Steven back.

Later, after we got into bed, I told him all about the old soccer ball and the TV shows, and the jeans with patches. I even told him about Ms. Hardy and Grandma.

I told him I didn't *really* mind. "I guess I'll get older sometime," I said.

Steven was just about asleep, but then he opened his eyes. "Sometimes Grandma calls me David," he said.